QUOTATIONS FROM

Chairman Jean

Bob van Wegen & Ron Wood

Red Deer Press

The Publishers
Red Deer Press
813 MacKimmie Library Tower
2500 University Drive N.W.
Calgary Alberta Canada T2N 1N4

Credits
Cover design and illustration by Rob Jobst
Text design by Dennis Johnson
Printed and bound in Canada by Friesens for Red Deer Press

National Library of Canada Cataloguing in Publication Data
Chrétien, Jean, 1934–
Quotations from Chairman Jean
ISBN 0-88995-239-6
1. Chrétien, Jean, 1934– —Quotations. 2. Canada—Politics and government—1993– —Humor. 3. Prime ministers—Canada—Quotations. I. Van Wegen, Bob, 1966– II. Wood, Ron, 1942– III. Title.
FC636.C47A5 2001 971.064'8'092 C2001-910214-3
F1034.3.C47A3 2001

5 4 3 2 1

Introduction

"Canada is at a turning point in its history, and it's not the time to send buffoons to the House of Commons to represent French Canadians."
Chrétien: The Will to Win, 1995

So declared a young Liberal named Jean Chrétien in 1963. Although more than fifty percent of voters agreed with him, he won his seat anyway.

Since then, the Right Honourable Chairman Jean has been a part of our lives. But who is this Shawinigan Colossus astride the political landscape?

He was born in La Baie Shawinigan on January 11, 1934. Rising from modest roots, he believed he had a great destiny, but instead he became a lawyer and went into politics. His political career, spanning five decades and two millennia, would take him to every corner of Canada, every corner of the world, and once a year to Vero Beach, Florida.

In 1963, the Towering Populist of the Prairies, Dief the Chief, was collapsing, and good Liberals everywhere saw an opportunity to regain what was rightfully theirs. Into this maelstrom crept Le Petite Gar de Shawinigan.

Even at this tender stage in his political career, he followed his instincts and went where the money was. The future Chairman rose through the ranks as Parliamentary Secretary to the Prime Minister, Minister of State for Finance and Minister of National Revenue. Just as John Kennedy had called on Americans to "ask what you can do for your country," Jean Chrétien inspired Canadians to do their duty: "The Canadian taxpayers . . . must bear their part of the burden and . . . they should be happy to do so."

When Chairman Trudeau took Canada's reins, our Jean became Minister of Indian Affairs and Northern Development, where his proposals for bringing aboriginals into the Canadian mainstream inspired few. "I still have my scalp," he said as he staggered from that portfolio.

The 1970s was a time of disco and discontent. Our future Chairman braved the decade as President of the Treasury Board, Minister of Industry, Trade and Commerce, and finally as Minister of Finance. When government spending quadrupled and the debt tripled, he was there to reassure us: "We have brought our own spending under effective control." And he offered sage advice on dealing with inflation: "If cabbage is too expensive for you, buy something else."

Barely interrupted by the apocryphal government of Joe Clark, Jean Chrétien became Minister of Justice, Attorney General, Minister of State for Social Development and minister in charge of constitutional negotiations under the renewed Trudeau Chairmanship. His arms were considerably lengthened by carrying all those portfolios, but all the better to reach out to Canadians.

During this time, one great accomplishment of the future Chairman was his negotiation of the Charter of Rights and Freedoms with reluctant premiers. "I'm going to clobber you," he cautioned. Our Jean prevailed, and today every single Canadian—man, woman and child—has the right to be ticked off by Supreme Court rulings.

Chrétien was Minister of Energy, Mines and Resources when Chairman Trudeau ventured out on a dark night to look up at His heavens and, mistaking snowflakes for stars, concluded His universe was not unfolding as it should. So it was that in 1984 Le Petite Gar de Shawinigan made his first attempt to become Ultimate Chairman. But when the music stopped, a pretender—John Turner—had the Chair. And later that year Brian Mulroney drove the Liberals into the dark.

As another Chairman might have said, the continuation of every great journey must begin with a single step. On February 27, 1986, Jean Chrétien resigned from the House of Commons and began his trek through the wilderness of law firms and corporate boards, cushioned only by the harsh comforts of large paycheques.

The Long March ended on June 23, 1990, when he was anointed Leader of All Liberals in a place unknown to Liberals called Calgary. Soon he was back in the House of Commons only two sword-lengths from the Ultimate Chair soon to be vacated by Mulroney and warmed fleetingly by Kim Campbell.

In the pivotal 1993 election, our Jean inflamed the masses against free trade, against the GST, against massive spending cuts, and he called for integrity and ethics in government. The revived Chairman, once dismissed as "yesterday's man," would show tomorrow a thing or two! As he said on the campaign trail, "It will be just like the good old days!" (*Western Report,* September 27, 1993)

So it was that on October 25, 1993, the Revolution was

complete, and Jean Chrétien was finally Chairman. One in a row. He soon introduced his realm to the benefits of free trade and used the GST and cuts to health care spending to slay the horrible deficit.

In 1997, settled firmly into the cushion of his Chair, the little guy from Shawinigan charged into an early election and returned as Chairman and Member of Parliament for St-Maurice, where voters were willing to return a quick prophet knowing a quick profit could be turned. Two in a row. In his second term as Chairman, he demonstrated that billion-dollar boondoggles, scandals and other trifles are mere bumps on the path to a better future for us all.

He called a millennial election in the autumn of 2000. Now, having won a hat trick of elections in the third period of his political life, the Chairman looks toward a tenure in office as endless as the gratitude of Canadians is boundless. Indeed, it is whispered that the Prime Minister's chair has permanently molded itself to his twin imprints, as if in silent tribute to a man who can truly sit.

This is the life and legend of the Ultimate Chairman in his own words, a lightweight guide to a political heavyweight and a testament to why incoherence in both official languages poses no barrier to success. Whether he's strangling protestors or throttling the language, putting pepper in our eyes or on our plate, Chairman Jean is our most misunderstood Prime Minister—literally. Does he flip-flop, or is he just flexible? Does he speak both official languages, or neither? Does he commit hilarious verbal gaffes, or are our two official languages simply inadequate to express his genius? You decide. We thank you for your purchase. The Chairman thanks you for the GST.

THE CHAIRMAN

On THE CHAIRMAN

"I have no great vision. I'm a realist. I don't see cities of a million under plexiglass domes in the next generation."
Chrétien: The Will to Win, 1995

On speaking to the common masses

"For me to speak good English was not a problem for me, in fact I enjoy it was a kind, perhaps silly on my part, but the more I was making mistakes in English, Aline will tell that to me all the time, I felt that I was with the average Canadian. 'Jean you're right there.' The majority of Canadians have an accent anyway. So, but it was a shortcoming. I should have been more meticulous. . . . But it was a way for me to be part of this. That, and today, especially in the intellectual, intelligentsia in Quebec, because I would speak a language that communicate very well with you, you know, the east end of Montreal, they look down on me. There's much more people living in east end Montreal than in Outremont."

Winnipeg Free Press, January 19, 1993

"I could have become a snob and talked *à la francaise.* I didn't want to. . . . You know, I am not faking it with anybody. . . . It is easy to put some mascara over the body, but I want the people to know who I am."
Chrétien: The Will to Win, 1995

"Am I the only one around here with half a brain."
Saturday Night, November 1997

On campaigning for the Liberal leadership

"I know politics better than the others and I'm better organized. . . . I have a lot of energy. I am minister of energy."
Sault Star, April 1984

On the Liberals' practice of alternating English and French leaders, which led to John Turner succeeding Pierre Trudeau

"I'm born on the wrong side of the river. If my name is John Christian and I was born in Ontario, I'd have a chance."
Chrétien: The Will to Win, 1995

On the comment that he reads only magazines and newspapers, not books

"I never ask anybody, 'What did you read last week?' It is an element of snobbism to discuss that."
Maclean's, October 18, 1993

On Bilingualism

"Bilingualism is a cheap price to pay for keeping Canadians united."
Treasury Board News Release, April 14, 1976

On a member of parliament opposed to official bilingualism

"I am proud to say I am a better Canadian than he is for being able to speak both languages."
Hansard, August 12, 1964

On learning ancient Greek and French as a schoolboy

"Why not . . . do like these people do and make sure that everybody who graduated from universities in Canada will be [like] a European living in North America. . . . Why not, we had to do that when we were kids."
St. John's Evening Telegram, June 10, 1991

On French immigration to Canada

"I am addressing the French directly to tell them: 'We need you.' . . . We hope to get more French-speaking immigrants because the birth rate of francophones is enormously reduced. It used to be, when they came, they had many kids; we called it the revenge of the baby-cribs."

Paris Match, quoted in the *National Post,* June 14, 2000

On the desire to rewrite Canadian history

"[I] would have preferred that Canada hadn't been conquered long ago by the British, that America remained French. But you don't rewrite history."

Le Monde, quoted in the *Toronto Star,* December 1, 1994

"I was not there [at the Plains of Abraham] when Montcalm was sleeping when Wolfe arrived in the middle of the night. If I'd been there, you know, it would have been different. I would have woken up Montcalm."

Globe and Mail, December 24, 1998

"You know, I wish too that the French had won against the English. . . . Of course, if the French had won, you know, Canada would speak French only and probably the U.S. too."

Remarks at Duke University, North Carolina, quoted on *CBC Sunday Report,* December 3, 2000

On intervening in the operations of PetroCanada in both official languages

"I discussed the problem of bilingual signs two months ago with the President of PetroCanada and I said then that I wanted services in Quebec to be offered in both official languages, the same as everywhere else in Canada."
Hansard, May 19, 1983

"Everyone knows I do not intervene in the operation of PetroCanada on a daily basis. It is managed like any other company."
Hansard, June 9, 1983

On Quebec Separatism

"I believe we should not give too much importance to that situation. . . . I am confident that movement is not serious."
Maiden Speech, House of Commons, May 23, 1963

On the Charlottetown Accord, which was defeated in Quebec and most of the rest of Canada

"[The Charlottetown Accord] should sell in Quebec. I expect the separatists to say it will be no good. Nothing will be good for them until they get what they want."
Saskatoon StarPhoenix, July 9, 1992

On the chances of the Bloc Quebecois becoming the Official Opposition (less than a year before it happened)

"Those movements last longer than roses but generally they have a limited lifespan."
Toronto Star, August 12, 1992

On the chances of the Parti Quebecois' defeating Daniel Johnson's Liberals (five months before it happened)

"What I am telling you today, the [financial] markets should listen to what I say because I know a little bit more politics than they do, normally. . . . We don't know the result of the election but there are a lot of people who are speculating [Premier Daniel Johnson] will not win. . . . All of you people [in the media] speculated for weeks and months that I was to [be] clobbered and here I am. . . . I don't lose my cool about the speculation in the press about the results of the election in Quebec."

Toronto Star, April 8, 1994

On the federalist victory by one-half of one percent in the 1995 Quebec referendum on separation

"Of course, the referendum did not produce as good a result as we expected, but we won and it's two–nothing. So, in a series like that, two–nothing—you're in a good position."

Canada AM, CTV, December 27, 1995

On Quebec Opposition Leader Daniel Johnson's warning that Jean Chrétien could be Canada's last prime minister if he didn't take unity problems more seriously

"I don't get involved in replying to this question; I do my job as prime minister, that's all."

Toronto Star, June 4, 1996

On rethinking that comment later the same day

"I will not be the last prime minister of Canada. Canada will stay together."

Toronto Star, June 4, 1996

On continuing to hold referendums

"It's getting a joke. It's not a suit a country that you put on and take off."

1997 election campaign, quoted in *Saturday Night,* November 1997

On the Parti Quebecois idea to ask Quebecers if they are a people

"Now they want to have an even more softer question. So now it is: 'Are you people?' I don't know, perhaps tomorrow it will be: 'Do you like apple pie?'"

Ottawa Sun, November 30, 1997

"For me, I don't think that Quebecers want to separate. . . . You know, the [referendum] question was, 'You keep the passports, you keep the citizenship, you keep the money, you keep the economic union and the political union.' It's somewhat what they've got now."

Ottawa Citizen, December 8, 1997

On the future of Canada without Quebec and vice versa

"If Canada is divisible, Quebec is divisible."
Victoria Times Colonist, January 30, 1996

"If Quebec goes, it's a question of years. . . . I think English Canada will eventually be absorbed by the United States."
Toronto Star, March 18, 1992

"If the Quebec dollar is worth as much as Canada's, don't worry; you can play golf in Florida until you die. But if the Quebec dollar is worth half the Canadian dollar, then buy cross-country skis right away."
Toronto Star, March 18, 1992

"One night when driving my car, I noticed that Radio-Canada [Quebec's CBC service] was no longer playing the national anthem of Canada. I reported that to the vice-president of the CBC. He confirmed this and said that 'O Canada' had not been played on Radio-Canada for three months. He told me that this was a technical error, to which I replied, 'My eye!' . . . At the time, the Parti Quebecois was elected in Quebec. I do not think it was a technical error that Radio-Canada had not played the anthem of my country for three months. . . . Since that time, they have started playing it again, and I am grateful for that."
Hansard, February 25, 1997

On the Bloc Quebecois blaming the Chairman for Lucien Bouchard's failure to get a meeting with Mexican President Ernesto Zedillo

"We know that the PQ's systematic plan is to humiliate itself in order to win a referendum that they will never win if they have the courage to ask a clear question to the people of Quebec. Why be pains in the asses to foreigners and not keep our problems here?"

Calgary Herald, May 7, 1999

On Bloc Quebecois leader Gilles Duceppe running again for Canadian Parliament

"Obviously this is a big failure for you because this is the third time you've come back for election."

Leaders' Debate, quoted by the Canadian Press, November 9, 2000

On Gilles Duceppe's claim that the Chairman's vision of Quebec isn't shared by Quebecers

"I'm as much a Quebecer as you are."

Leaders' Debate, quoted by the Canadian Press, November 9, 2000

On Race Relations

"Whether we as Canadians want to admit it or not, racism is alive and well in Canada. We have a problem here that must be dealt with."
Toronto Star, May 12, 1992

On declining to criticize his Chief of Staff, Jean Pelletier, who told the media that he didn't think a black person could be elected in Quebec City

"Everyone is welcome in the Liberal party in all parts of Canada."

Toronto Star, February 10, 1993

On the contribution made by black members of parliament, including Ovide Jackson, Hedy Fry, Senator Anne Cools and Jean Augustine, who, he pointed out, walks behind him on the way to Question Period

"They smile a lot."

Ottawa Sun, February 18, 1996

On Philippine-born Rey Pagtakhan, Secretary of State for Asia Pacific, at a show-and-tell on Canadian multiculturalism during a trade mission in Shanghai, China

"He look a bit like a Chinese."

Calgary Sun, February 15, 2001

On Aboriginal Affairs

"I was the only Minister of Indian Affairs to have survived six years at that posting while managing to keep my scalp."
Ottawa Citizen, September 8, 1990

On the appropriateness of that remark when asked about it later

Question: "You mentioned the scalps and it was perhaps funny when you were Minister of Indian Affairs, but at this time, nobody found it at all amusing. Do you think that you're a bit rusty?"

Chrétien: "We spent an hour, an hour and a half in discussion with the Native peoples . . . and when I made this joke, everybody thought it was quite funny . . . so I don't think it ruffled anybody's feathers."
Interview transcript, 1990

On the Oka crisis

"What is Mulroney doing to our country, when we reach the stage where we see the Canadian army pointing rifles at our first citizens?"

Toronto Star, September 16, 1990

Question: "Would you have used the army against the natives at Oka?"

Chrétien: "I would have had no choice in that file because the premier of the province requested the Armed Forces. . . . You know it was sacred ground for them, and they were to cut trees who are there for them since centuries, and you know they were to be cut to permit a few bourgeois to play golf."

Question Period, CTV, September 30, 1990

On aboriginal peoples' financial accountability while the future Chairman was Minister of Indian Affairs and Northern Development

"We want to do something. However, we cannot spend millions of dollars without developing some criteria and rules for the administration of those moneys. . . . They would like to have money for which they will not be accountable. As a Minister of the Crown, I cannot accept that concept. We should sign agreements with the Indians but they should be treated like other people. They should provide us with the accounts we require after they have received the money. . . . I think that when we are contracting with any organization in the land we should apply the same financial rules as to all other organizations."

Hansard, November 24, 1971

On THE CONSTITUTION

"We should be rejoicing. We have a completely new Canada. We are completely independent for the first time in our history. We should be happy we achieved it with a great consensus."
Windsor Star, November 12, 1981

On the constitution being repatriated without the consent of Quebec

"I've always been for a Quebec constitutional veto."
Montreal Gazette, June 9, 1984

On the gentle art of persuading provincial ministers to accept the Charter of Rights and Freedoms

"I circulated among the provincial ministers to pressure them into shifting their positions [on the Charter of Rights and Freedoms]. 'You know, you guys,' I said, 'there's going to be a referendum. I don't want one and you don't want one. But I'm telling you, I'm going to go into your provinces, and I'm going to say you're opposed to freedom of religion and equality of women and all that. And I'm going to clobber you.'"

Straight from the Heart, 1985

On the Meech Lake Accord and the attempt to repair the constitutional rift with Quebec (comments made while on sabbatical from politics)

"The premiers staged a power grab for themselves, not for the people. They will destroy the national will."

Saskatoon StarPhoenix, April 4, 1988

On the Meech Lake Accord giving Quebec francophones too much clout in deciding the fate of language policy in Canada

"There are a million francophones outside Quebec. . . . Acadians are more French than we are in Quebec."

New Brunswick Telegraph Journal, March 12, 1990

On consulting Quebecers about the Calgary Declaration, a unity package posed by nine federalist premiers

"We are not saying that we will not hold consultations in Quebec but at the same time we are not saying that we will."

Hansard, November 19, 1997

On the sensitive issue of Canadian unity during the opening days of a Quebec provincial election campaign

"The list of Quebec's traditional demands have been met. . . . The Constitution should not be a general store."

Globe and Mail, October 26, 1998

On accusations that his statement helped Lucien Bouchard's Parti Quebecois defeat Jean Charest's Liberals

"But, what I did, at this moment, is I talked about all the changes that have been made by agreement [rather than by constitutional change]. I have the list here. During the campaign, Mr. Bouchard said that this list—I should take the credit. . . . There's only one change in the Constitution. So, if you read the whole interview, all of it . . . it was what I am telling you today. And the reality is that Mr. Charest might have said something at this time, at that time, but look, he got more votes than all of you predicted. So, for me, I have this meeting called since a long time. *La Presse* wanted to have an article for October . . . and I kept my word. . . . The way it was interpreted, it was very—and some people were making comments not having read the transcript. And for me, I always say there is a technique that is working. One problem at the time. . . . You don't know how happy I was when I saw Mr. Bouchard taking the credit of my work."

Ottawa Citizen, December 5, 1998

On the prospect of Canada becoming a republic

"I've got enough problems with the separatists in Quebec; I don't want problems with the monarchists in Nova Scotia. . . . I don't think guys are stopping the hockey game in the tavern to discuss the monarchy."

Globe and Mail, December 24, 1998

On THE AMERICANS

"I like to stand up to the Americans. It's popular. But you have to be careful because they're our friends."
Ottawa Citizen, September 26, 1998

On whether Bill Clinton was distracted from his duties by the Monica Lewinsky scandal

"I don't know. I don't say he's not doing his job. You know, I just say that if he's not bothered by that, that is good. My view is I've got other problems to face than he faces. But I know, talking to other leaders—I talk to other leaders—and read what they have to say. You saw what Mandela said. What Helmet Kohl said . . . and others. So, they are preoccupied, but it is a problem. For me, I am an ally [of the United States].

Ottawa Citizen, September 26, 1998

On a question about illegal drugs coming over the border from Canada to the United States

"It's more trade."
Montreal Gazette, April 9, 1997

On being told by President Clinton that he had heard the question incorrectly

"I heard 'trucks.' . . . I'm sorry."
Montreal Gazette, April 9, 1997

On the American media's failure to cover Canadian affairs

"Canada. You don't write much about Canada unfortunately. We are a favourite client for you than Japan. You know, you buy—we buy more and you sell more to us than you do with Japan. Very seldom you talk about Canada. Canada is virtually ignored by the press in the United States. So much, that they had a survey of one time and they asked whoever it is the prime minister of Canada, and one and a half per cent knew the name. . . . So you know we are in a very turbulent world at this moment. You do whatever you want."
Ottawa Citizen, September 26, 1998

On the Machiavellian art of international affairs, including Bill Clinton's reasons for approving three new NATO members (comments made to Belgian Prime Minister and caught on open microphone at a NATO summit)

"It's not for reasons of security. It's all done for short-term political reasons to win elections."

Toronto Star, July 8, 1997

On Canadian troops going to Haiti (comments caught on open microphone at a NATO summit)

"Haiti. [Clinton] goes to Haiti with soldiers. The next year, Congress doesn't allow him to go back. So he phones me. Okay, I send my soldiers, and then afterwards, I ask for something else in exchange."

Toronto Star, July 8, 1997

On American politicians and the U.S. political system (comments caught on open microphone at a NATO summit)

"In your country and my country all the [American] politicians would be in prison because they sell their votes. 'You want me to vote on NATO? Then you have to build me a bridge in my constituency.' That's what's unbelievable."

Toronto Star, July 8, 1997

On maintaining Canadian trade surpluses with Americans by encouraging them to think of Canada as a backward rural cousin

"If you live in Chicago, you don't know if you're getting natural gas from Texas or Alberta; it smells the same."
Globe and Mail, January 27, 1986

"The trade between Canada and United States is much bigger than the trade of United States with Japan, and Europe, and we have a large surplus but nobody knows it in the United States and don't tell them."
Remarks at Duke University, North Carolina, December 3, 2000

On being a model political leader

"Bill [Clinton] thinks of me like a big brother. He often says: 'Jean was an MP when I was in college, Prime Minister when I was in University, and he will still be Prime Minister when I am retired.' . . . It was a nice thing to say on his part. He says Canada is a model for the U.S. . . . [Bill and Hillary] would like to follow us in health care and, most of all, our gun control legislation."
Paris Match, quoted in the *National Post,* June 19, 2000

"Bill thinks of me like a big brother."

On Military Base Closures

"If they have to cut in the national defence, they should not cut in areas like here. . . . A base right in Toronto could have easily been cut to spare impending closings in Moncton and Summerside, P.E.I."
New Brunswick Telegraph Journal,
February 5, 1990

On military base closures before a federal election

"A federal Liberal government would not have targeted the military base here [at Portage La Prairie] for closure."
Globe and Mail, September 8, 1990

On military base closures after winning the election

"But we tried to be fair and I know it caused pain. Just to give you an example, we have to close military bases in almost every province, in the poor provinces like Nova Scotia we closed bases. In Chatham, New

Brunswick, in the riding of the prime minister, the premier of that province, we close the base. It's not easy to do. In St-Jean, Quebec, in Downsview, in Ontario. In Calgary, in Ottawa, and here in British Columbia too."

Liberal fundraiser, Vancouver, October 2, 1997

On Atlantic Canada

"Civilization is better here than in Montreal or Toronto in many ways. People are not aggressive. When I campaign in the big cities I meet a problem every hour."
New Brunswick Telegraph Journal,
November 21, 1990

On the impact of federal budget cuts in Atlantic Canada

"But what counts is that we did the right thing. . . . Because you were depending on the federal government more than others, naturally the price had to be higher."
Ottawa Citizen, October 11, 1997

On the impact of federal budget cuts in Atlantic Canada while exchanging views with Canadian voters during a CBC TV/Radio Canada Town Hall Meeting

Juanita MacKeigen, Louisbourg, Nova Scotia: "I live in Cape Breton. We have an official [unemployment] rate of 23 percent and a real rate that's higher than that. What I would like to know is how you sleep at night knowing that there is people and workers in Atlantic Canada that live every day with these statistics."

Chrétien: "Some people will always live in Cape Breton and some initiatives—some people, some entrepreneurs will create some jobs."

MacKeigen: "Excuse me, but wouldn't you have to have money to start a business?"

CBC TV, December 10, 1996

On forgetting to mention Employment Insurance reforms during a speech in New Brunswick, where he talked about the Internet, funding for the arts and the CBC, the national debt, taxes, medical research, bilingualism, Acadian culture and the western Canada-based Canadian Alliance party's policies on medicare and decentralization

"I'm not perfect, I admit it. . . . I wanted to talk about it but I had forgotten."

Victoria Times Colonist, November 5, 2000

On the topic of Employment Insurance when reminded to return to the microphone

"We have realized it was not a good move that we made, in a sense. We should [not have made the EI cuts] in retrospect. We had a huge problem and everybody had to pay a price to help us."

Canadian Press, November 4, 2000

On Equality of the Provinces

"With all due respect, Prince Edward Island is not as important as Quebec."
Charlottetown Guardian, June 4, 1990

On all things being equal

"I am for the equality of citizens, and I am for the equality of the people of Canada. I have been for that all the time I have been in Canada."
Hansard, September 24, 1997

"The Leader of the Opposition wanted me to speak about equality of the provinces. I am for that."
Hansard, September 25, 1997

Senate Reform

"The regions of Canada need to be more involved in decision-making and policy-making at the national level. To meet the hopes and dreams of those who live in the west and the Atlantic, a reformed Senate is essential. It must be a Senate that is elected, effective and equitable."
Hansard, September 24, 1991

On a Triple-E Senate—Elected, Effective, Equal

"Canadians as a whole want to have elected representatives. Once that has been accomplished, some say that we have to have the same number of Senators per province, that P.E.I. should have the same number of Senators that Ontario has. I am convinced that is not going to be acceptable."
Winnipeg Free Press, January 24, 1990

"You want the Triple-E Senate and I want one too."
Toronto Star, February 2, 1990

"The Liberal government in two years will make [the Senate] elected. . . . As prime minister I can take steps to make it happen."

Edmonton Journal, October 14, 1990

On a Triple-E Senate six years later

"I will name a senator who I will choose and who will represent my party in the House of Commons."

Hansard, May 9, 1996

On rejecting elected senators while patronage-appointing 19 Liberals in a row to the Senate

"The prime minister of the land is obliged to respect the Constitution for Alberta and all the provinces of Canada."

Ottawa Citizen, November 6, 1997

On being asked if Alberta's election to choose two Senate nominees is "a joke"

"Of course."

Calgary Herald, September 17, 1998

On defending the status quo in the Senate

"We have a Senate that is not elected. We on this side

voted for an elected, equal and effective Senate while the Leader of the Opposition campaigned against the Charlottetown Accord. We have a Senate that has been given to us by the Brits. It is like the House of Lords. And here I am, a French Canadian from Quebec, defending a British tradition."

Hansard, October 20, 1998

On an increase in the unreformed Senate's $450-million budget

"When there will be a very large consensus we might act [to reform the Senate], but at this moment what is important is that the Senate is doing its job and doing it well."

Calgary Sun, March 5, 1999

On how the Senate really costs taxpayers nothing

"When you take one Member of Parliament from the House of Commons to the Senate do you realize you save money? If I appoint you in the Senate I pay you full pay. If I appoint an MP I pay his full pay but he doesn't draw a pension. If he goes back home he gets his pension and you still have the full pay [for the person filling the Senate position]. If you don't have these people in the job you have somebody else. . . . It is costing the taxpayer nothing."

Globe and Mail, August 1, 1984

On Patronage

"You appoint people of your party. I'm not going to name people who are not Liberals. It's the way the British gave to us."
Kitchener–Waterloo Record, July 23, 1997

On Pierre Trudeau's patronage appointment of 17 Liberals in one day at the end of his term, which helped sink the campaign of Liberal John Turner

"You know, at that time, we named, at the end of a regime, a number of members who were competent to serve in the jobs. . . . There was only one that was questioned in terms of abilities, and they were not under investigation. I always said that someone who has served Parliament for 20 years, if he can fill a job and he has the competence to do it, after he has enough of public life, there's nothing wrong to use those talents who got elected before in jobs that they can serve . . . and none of them have turned out to be people who cannot fill the jobs that were given to them. Some, for health reasons,

eventually resigned, but . . . there was a debate about their abilities or incapacities to serve."
Ottawa Citizen, February 2, 1990

"I'm not interested in patronage because I'm a Liberal."
Ottawa Citizen, February 2, 1990

On patronage and conflict of interest after appointing an old law firm colleague to the Supreme Court

"I have informed the House that I have never been a partner in that law firm. I worked two or three days a week in the law firm and was paid for my services. I had nothing to do with the management of the firm. I was never a partner and I did not know anything about the relationship among any of the lawyers in the firm."
Hansard, October 1, 1997

On the legal interpretation of part of the failed Charlottetown Accord

"I am not a lawyer."
December 20, 1994, quoted in the *Edmonton Sun,* April 14, 2000

On the Banks

"They are very fat. Just look at their buildings in Toronto."
Montreal Gazette, April 26, 1984

On the difference between business and banking

"They are not hurting and they are very sanctimonious. . . . They are the ones who invested in Dome [Petroleum]. We did not bail out Dome; we bailed out the banks. An owner of a company, if he fails, he loses everything; the banks have no problem."
Montreal Gazette, April 26, 1984

On the decision to prohibit the merger of the Royal Bank and the Bank of Montreal

Question: "Do you agree with the decision on the bank merger?"
Chrétien: "Absolutely."
Question: "Why is that?"

Chrétien: "Because it's a good decision."
Question: "Why do you think it's a good decision?"
Chrétien: "Because it's the best decision."
Question: "Why?"
Chrétien: "Because it's a good decision."
Question: "Is there a reason?"
Chrétien: "Because they did not make a case and Mr. Martin gave the reason why the government decided not to proceed."

December 14, 1998, exchange with ISN-TV reporter Shaun Poulter, quoted in the *Ottawa Citizen,* January 9, 1999

On Spending Public Money

"Trudeau mentioned to me that the National Gallery wanted to buy a masterpiece by the great Italian painter, Lotto . . . and it needed a million dollars from the Treasury Board. 'Is that Lotto-Quebec or Lotto-Canada?' I joked, but I got the message and the National Gallery got the painting."
Straight from the Heart, 1985

On the Chrétien cabinet's increased use of corporate jets

"The ministers are just using the facility to make sure that they can get the message to the people."
Globe and Mail, March 20, 1996

On using a government jet to attend a secret Grits-only golf day with Atlantic premiers at a golf course that had recently undergone a taxpayer-funded facelift

"I've been here many times and I wanted to see the improvement of the golf course."
Montreal Gazette, August 19, 1997

On a federal government grant of $19,000 to buy golf balls for a Maritime golf course

"It is an area of Canada that needs economic development. . . . To modernize a golf course a bit for tourists to visit one of the most beautiful parts of Canada which . . . has some economic problems, I think the Reform Party should compliment the government."

Ottawa Sun, September 27, 1997

On a federal government arts grant to study medieval music

"To be knowledgeable about great ancient music is very important for some people in Canada. . . . I'm not an expert but I love Gregorian music. It was part of the services in the Catholic Church when I was a kid."

Ottawa Sun, September 27, 1997

On announcing a $500-million grant for Toronto waterfront development two days before the federal election

"I did not want to make this announcement at this time because some people will say that it is too close to an election. . . . But Mel [Mayor Mel Lastman] called me and said, 'I needed badly to win in the municipal election.' So I said: 'Mel, buddy, OK.'"

Canadian Press, October 20, 2000

On Political Integrity

"I have been in public life for a long time and my integrity has never been challenged."
Ottawa Sun, March 19, 1998

On taking pride in personal integrity

"Look at my record. . . . In terms of integrity, I'm very proud that I've been a Member of Parliament for 25 years and a minister for 18 years and never has anybody been able to question my integrity."
Ottawa Citizen, April 6, 1993

On refusing to disclose the Ethics Counsellor's advice regarding a minister who was being pressured to resign

"[The Ethics Counsellor] was consulted yesterday and he gave his advice. The advice he gave was given to me and it did not force me to change my mind about the decision I took a few days ago."
Hansard, October 28, 1994

On the rest of the Chairman's ministers

"My ministers, I don't look into their private life, as long as they don't do anything that is against the law. . . . Morality is their own personal problem."

Globe and Mail, December 24, 1998

On the claim that the Airbus scandal was politically motivated to smear former Prime Minister Mulroney

"It is, moreover, my duty as Prime Minister to ensure that police inquiries can be carried out without any political interference by anyone whatsoever."

Hansard, June 14, 1996

On Being MP for St-Maurice

"You know, I even phoned a judge."
Maclean's, May 3, 1976

On contacting a judge on behalf of a constituent

"It was crazy—all those guys on the other side [of the House] acting like offended virgins. When I called the judge I said, 'I'm Jean Chrétien, member for St-Maurice.' . . . Well, when I became a minister I was not any the less the member for St-Maurice."
Maclean's, May 3, 1976

On lobbying the head of the government-owned Business Development Bank on behalf of the owner of a troubled hotel in St-Maurice (The owner had purchased the inn from the Chairman and his partners in 1993, and the Chairman still had an interest in the neighboring golf course. The new hotel owner had been denied a loan, but eventually received $615,000.

The Ethics Counsellor said the Chairman didn't break any rules, but he also admitted there weren't any rules.)

"You know, you call who you know. . . . I know the president [of BDC] so I called him once or twice. He came to visit me at my home with a group one day. Fine. It's the normal operation."

Montreal Gazette, November 17, 2000

On being questioned about the scandal while in China

"We discuss that in Ottawa. Okay. No problem. Next?"

National Post, February 16, 2001

On absolution granted by voters in the 2000 election

"They are files that they have been asking questions on for months, even before the election. And since then, Canadians have pronounced themselves."

National Post, February 17, 2001

On Deborah Grey's persistent questioning about a $600,000 government employment grant to another hotel in his St-Maurice riding and a $5,000 donation by the hotel chain's parent company to the federal Liberal Party

"Shut up."

Ottawa Sun, October 8, 1997

"I have been a Member of Parliament since 1963 and I have always done my job in a proper way."
National Post, October 18, 2000

On a St-Maurice road construction contract being awarded to a constituent rather than a lower bidder from the Quebec City area

"In all honesty I can say I would prefer that the contract go to a fellow in my own riding. . . . What do you say after you say you're not sorry?"
Maclean's, May 3, 1976

On being an effective Member of Parliament (Between 1996 and 2000, companies in the Chairman's riding received $8.5 million in funding from Human Resources Development Canada—more than Manitoba, Saskatchewan and Alberta combined.)

"I will not apologize to anybody to do my job as a member for St-Maurice."
National Post, November 21, 2000

"What do you say after you say you're not sorry?"

On Billion-Dollar Boondoggles

"Just look at the way the Tories are spending money. . . . If it were a Keystone Cops movie, you might laugh. But taxpayers must feel like crying. Liberals are committed to scrutinizing government expenditure. Government can no longer afford to waste taxpayers' money."
November 20, 1991, quoted in
the *Montreal Gazette,* March 16, 2000

On an internal audit revealing that the Chairman's government might have misspent over a billion dollars in Human Resources Development Canada's granting programs

"Administrative problems of this sort always exist. . . . These are problems of an administrative nature, as the Auditor General points out every year, and we adjust. . . . There is some explanation, perhaps, from the fact there is some devolution of decision-making in the regions in some cases . . . and we had to cut 20 percent of the bureaucrats when we decided to cut."

National Post, February 1, 2000

On the RCMP's investigation into about twenty grants, including several in the prime minister's riding

"It's not allegations of big fraud there."

February 2, 2000, quoted in the *Montreal Gazette,* March 16, 2000

On the whereabouts of Liberal members of parliament who failed to appear at the Auditor General's briefing on the boondoggle, which caused the meeting to be cancelled

"I don't know. . . . [The Chairman swats at a reporter's tape recorder.] Will you get out of my way please?"

Canadian Press, October 19, 2000

On swatting at the reporter's tape recorder

"I was going out and the stair was there. I said: 'Please get out of my way, I have to go home.'"

Canadian Press, October 20, 2000

On Robin Hood as a role model for the Chairman and Human Resources Development Canada after the Auditor General found that "controls had broken down, putting public funds at unacceptable risk"

"You must have a central government to get money from the rich areas to help those areas that need help. . . . Sometimes there are mistakes. When you find mistakes you correct them."

Canadian Press, November 9, 2000

On Debts and Deficits

"We have brought our own spending under effective control."
Speech to the Fifth Canadian Financial Conference,
Toronto, June 27, 1978

On the art of understatement—as program spending (not including debt charges) rose from $10.2 billion to $27.6 billion and the national debt rose from $34.8 billion to $55.4 billion between 1970–75

"During the years 1971, 1972, 1973 and 1974, governmental expenses may have been considerable, I agree. Of course, in general, the Progressive Conservatives say that we spend too much. However, the New Democrats say that we do not spend enough. But the Canadian people recognize that we always have a much more balanced judgement in these situations and we do not fall into one extreme or the other."

Hansard, May 9, 1975

On the art of restraint—as program spending rose from $27.6 billion to $35.7 billion and the national debt rose from $55.4 billion to $70.5 billion between 1975–77

"In a time of inflationary pressure, the government has decided to set an example of restraint. . . . To cut back the rate of growth, some planned expenditures must be cancelled. These cutbacks are not inconsistent with some growth."

Hansard, July 2, 1975

"I will continue to exercise the greatest possible degree of restraint. There will be considerable belt-tightening in Ottawa. I can assure you that all departments are aware of the sharp axe in the hands of the Treasury Board."

Speech to the Edmonton Chamber of Commerce, October 24, 1975

On criticism that a cut was "cosmetic" because his plans as Treasury Board President included increasing spending by "only" 16 percent compared to 28 percent the year before

"Well, you can buy a hell of a lot of lipstick and face powder with a billion and a half dollars."

Chrétien: The Will to Win, 1995

On the art of balance—as program spending rose from $35.7 billion to $42.9 billion and the national debt rose from $70.5 to $100.7 billion between 1977–79

"In considering the need for short-term action, I was determined not to let the federal deficit get away from us. Excessive action would not solve our economic problems. It would not have good results in psychological terms. And I was sure it would not be a solution in political terms either, because the people of Canada are looking today for discipline and responsible action."

Speech in Montreal, April 16, 1978

On criticism that the Liberals had more than septupled government spending to over $70 billion and more than quintupled the national debt to about $200 billion since 1970

"To seek to balance the books for the sake of balancing the books is to condemn hundreds of thousands of young people to the misery of unemployment, despair and lost hopes. That I shall not do."

London Free Press, March 21, 1984

"Those who would cut deficits for the sake of cutting deficits are going to push our unemployment levels higher."

Speech to the Council of Forest Industries, Vancouver, April 13, 1984

On the Conservatives' debt reduction record between 1984–93, which doubled the federal debt again

"[The Conservatives] were elected to reduce the debt, they made a promise to balance the books. . . . They started with $160 billion and they reduced it to $440 billion. What a reduction."

Toronto Star, April 4, 1993

On the deficit-elimination platform of the Reform Party

"Zero deficit is zero jobs. . . . There is more than money in life. There are human values."

Ottawa Sun, October 11, 1993

On the Chairman's success at balancing the budget by increasing taxes and cutting health care payments to the provinces by $6 billion per year

"We are way ahead of the Ontario government [on deficit-cutting], and we have managed to do that in a civilized way. It is the Liberal way."

Ottawa Sun, March 22, 1996

On Health Care

"I had a friend who went to Florida where he had a heart attack. When he saw his hospital bill, he had another."
Remarks at the 1978 Liberal convention,
Chrétien: The Will to Win, 1995

On federal transfer payments to the provinces while in Opposition

"I promised that [transfer payments for health care, education, etc.] will not go down, and I hope that we will be able to increase them. . . . I really do not intend to lower the level of transfer payments, not at all, below those which exist at the present time."

Leader's Debate, 1993 election

"Renegotiation of federal–provincial fiscal arrangements will be a major priority of a Liberal government. And our objective will be to achieve the maximum degree of predictability for both levels of government."

Speech at the Empire Club, Toronto, February 11, 1993

On Conservatives' cuts to federal transfer payments to the provinces

"Look at what the current [Conservative] government has done. To make its books look better, it cut billions in transfer payments to the provinces. The provinces then cut services and downloaded their deficits to municipalities. At the end of the day, it's still the same taxpayer stuck with the tab."

Speech at the Empire Club, Toronto, February 11, 1993

On cuts to federal transfer payments to the provinces upon becoming Chairman (These amounted to about $25 billion between 1994 and 2000.)

"But I say that for us, for example, you know, we have cut some transfer payments. . . . And we had to do that to restore the good finances of the nation."

CBC Radio, February 26, 1998

On provincial pleas to restore health care funding

"[The Premiers] say they should have all the money we have cut restored. I will tell the premiers the same thing, restore all your cuts and we will restore all the transfers."

Hamilton Spectator, December 15, 1998

"You know, we were working on the social union and suddenly it's become a question of money."

Ottawa Citizen, December 12, 1998

"Some mornings I want to give [the provinces] more money and the morning after I say no."

Calgary Herald, January 14, 1999

"There's no doubt about it, that they said themselves that they were to sign in blood that the money were to go to health if we were to give money. . . . And some who were willing to sign with blood are not now willing to sign with ink. So we have to clarify that."

Ottawa Citizen, January 16, 1999

"Family is a value that has to be promoted. We also need to make sure we aren't penalizing people in terms of tax because they have families. But I'm not a guy who makes promises before being elected."
Homemakers Magazine, May 1990

On declining to appoint a special ministry or royal commission to strengthen family life

"It's better to find solutions in the way politicians think."
Toronto Star, April 22, 1990

On pensions for homemakers, who *still* cannot contribute to the Canada Pension Plan

Question: "Would you be behind new programs like pensions for housewives?"
Chrétien: "Yes."
Question: "Where would the money come from, given the current state of the Canada Pension Plan?"

Chrétien: "We'll have to adjust according to the needs of the program. The money is there and it will have to be shared in a different fashion."

Toronto Sun, May 6, 1984

On gay marriages

"I'm not personally very comfortable with that because I don't know how that works in a society."

Toronto Star, October 17, 1996

On the Chairman's concern over whether CBC TV reporter Christina Lawand had ever benefited from the federal parental leave program

"No? Gee, it's time. . . . Cause you're a nice girl you know. . . . Because of the bad federal government, if you want a baby, madame, you will have six more [months of] leave paid by the federal government. . . . So take advantage of that generosity, mademoiselle."

Calgary Herald, June 10, 2000

On arms control in the home

"Why buy automatic rifles, nuclear arms, to have fun with? It's dangerous, and when they're in the house, there could be a child who will use that, and sometimes the family circumstances are not very happy, and they could use them."

May 1997, quoted in *Saturday Night,* November 1997

Taxation without Vexation

"Economics have no mystery. Every time the government spends money, it takes it out of the taxpayers' pockets. . . . We should be able to explain to the Canadian taxpayers that they must bear their part of the burden and that they should be happy to do so."
Hansard, February 19, 1968

On the Chairman's philosophy of taxation

"I think taxation is a system of redistribution of income, and taxes have to come from capital gains just as taxes come from personal gains."

Hansard, November 25, 1977

On across-the-board tax cuts

"I don't think it is the right thing to do in a society like Canada."

Globe and Mail, October 22, 1996

"Over the course of this mandate, we will pay down debt and will reduce taxes."

Confederation Dinner Speech, Toronto, November 6, 1997

On why the poor are better for the economy than the rich

"It's not charity. . . . When you give money or resources to the poor they spend their money. You know it's, they, they spend their money. To give great tax cuts to the rich, you're just increasing the savings, increasing the savings, but the poor spend their money and that's create a lot of activities in the economy."

Remarks at Duke University, North Carolina, December 3, 2000

On Sharing and the West

"Some Westerners, in their time of success, had forgotten the concept of sharing on which Canada had been built. They argued that their resources belonged to them and were not to be shared with the less fortunate parts of the country. Alberta accumulated an enormous trust fund for its citizens and howled when Ottawa tried to get some of the wealth for the rest of the nation."
Straight from the Heart, 1985

On ensuring that provinces' natural resource wealth is redistributed across the country

"Electricity, oil and other natural resources must be shared by all Canadians first and foremost. If we find we have enough, we can allow exports to other countries. This does not only apply to Alberta oil, but also to the hydroelectric resources that Quebec can produce."
Hansard, November 8, 1973

"We see in Canada, socialists in Saskatchewan trying to

set up Crown corporations to isolate the resource industry from federal taxation. I do not accept that kind of socialism which does not spread wealth across the land. . . . When Honourable Members rise in the House and talk about the poor, they should consider this particular aspect and then tell the government of Saskatchewan not to use this kind of scheme to hide profitable provincial industries from the tax collector of Canada."

Hansard, November 22, 1974

On the National Energy Program, which the Chairman championed, and through which energy-producing provinces "shared" more than $134 billion with the rest of Canada while enduring a decade-long economic slump

"The most vehement critics seemed to forget that federal money had poured into the West to alleviate the hard times of the 1930s, nor did they remember that the Liberals were defeated in 1957 for trying to build a pipeline to bring natural gas from the West to the Ontario market in order to generate Western prosperity."

Straight from the Heart, 1985

On the merits of the National Energy Program despite the disastrous economic downturn in the oil industry

Question: "Would you retain the National Energy Program?"

Chrétien: "Yes, I am for Canadianization, for self-sufficiency."

Question: "Oil is a very high risk enterprise involving a great deal of money. All the NEP seems to have done is let Canadians share in the risks and the losses and forfeit the profits we would have got through taxing private companies when they made money."

Chrétien: "No, because the oil companies paid very little taxes over the years, because they reinvested in drilling. We're getting our money now not out of taxing profits, we're getting our money out of taxing the oil. That's the difference. We tax the product, not the corporation."

Toronto Sun, May 6, 1984

On Energy Minister Jean's response to Chairman Trudeau's diversion of National Energy Program revenue to purposes other than those promised

"Yeah, it's shit. I know it's shit. And you know what happens when there's shit. They say, 'Hey, Jean, here's the shovel.'"

Chrétien: The Will to Win, 1995

On the workings of the National Energy Program

"Our policy is a mix of prices and all the components are not known. . . . Our policy will be a Canadian price, made in Canada, according to the cost in Canada. And there will be a mix in that price that will include the price of the old oil, the new oil, the tarsands and heavy oil. There is also a lot of talk about what they call tertiary recovery. Because of the oil formations, some of the oil is expensive to pump out so they leave it there. We'll try to have a price for every element of the oil produced in Canada plus the cost of the oil we import. We'll pull all the costs together and that will fix the price."

Winnipeg Free Press, February 14, 1980

On regulating energy prices at the retail level

"The federal government, with the producing provinces, controls only the wellhead price. We are not involved in setting the price in the retail market; that is done through market forces."

Hansard, June 22, 1983

On reconsidering the merits of the market when gas prices went up in Eastern Canada and the future Chairman was exiled to the Opposition benches by Brian Mulroney's election

"Will the Prime Minister [Brian Mulroney] tell the House why, in respect to the agreement with the Western provinces, it was not agreed to deregulate the price of natural gas and let the market forces decide the price? Every knowledgeable person in the field knows that if we have an agreement to deregulate the price of natural gas, the price for that resource paid by consumers in Eastern Canada will go down."

Hansard, April 1, 1985

On reconsidering the merits of the National Energy Program

"Energy policy must be clear and straightforward. It must be fair and non-discriminatory."

Calgary Herald, November 15, 1990

"I won't make the same mistake. I will not have a Canadian price to permit Ontario and Quebec to take the rest in revenue. . . . We could find another mechanism if we decided to, but certainly not to give room for taxation for the provincial government outside of Alberta."

New Brunswick Telegraph Journal, November 15, 1990

On being haunted by the National Energy Program years later

"The only NEP around Preston Manning is 'Negative Election Politics.'"

Calgary Herald, May 26, 1997

"Energy policy must be clear and straightforward."

On Energy and the Environment

"My English may not be very good, but my statement the other day applied to drilling offshore."
Hansard, March 14, 1974

On the finer points of environmental hazards associated with offshore drilling in the Arctic

Question: "Will the Minister explain why Imperial Oil was allowed to drill in the Beaufort Sea before environmental studies had been completed?"

Chrétien: ". . . This last drilling was done from an island, so it is not offshore drilling."

Question: "An artificial island?"

Chrétien: "It is not offshore, as far as I know. It was an island."

Question: May I point out that it was a man-made island, an artificial island?"

Chrétien: "It was an island. . . . I make a distinction between offshore drilling from a platform or from a ship and drilling from man-made islands which are a very safe device approved by all the experts."

Hansard, March 14, 1974

"I argued in Cabinet saying that drilling from ships was safer than drilling from man-made islands and ice platforms, which the exploration companies already had permission to do."

Straight from the Heart, 1985

On Liberals and the West

"Ontario has been the main beneficiary of Confederation, and as a result there will always be some tension between it and the West."
Straight from the Heart, 1985

On staying in touch with Alberta

"I had occasion to call Mr. Merv Leitch [the Treasurer of Alberta] . . . to indicate that we wanted to cut the sales tax of the province. He indicated that they did not have a sales tax. Thus, my proposition was not feasible."
Hansard, June 13, 1978

On the financial losses of western farmers resulting from a grain handlers strike

Chrétien: "The producer will not lose very much."
Some Hon. Members: "Oh, oh!"
Chrétien: "The producer will not lose very much because . . ."

Some Hon. Members: "Oh, oh!"
Chrétien: "Wait a minute. I am no expert; I do not know."
Some Hon. Members: "Oh, oh!"
Chrétien: "They have not lost their wheat. Perhaps the price will be better next summer and they will be grateful; I do not know. I just say that they are like anybody else."
Hansard, March 19, 1975

On the problems of farmers

"When you look at the future of agriculture, you realize that food will become very important in the years to come."
Saturday Night, November 1997

On seeking the support of cranky western malcontents

"I recognize that Western Canadians have often felt that the Liberal Party was out of touch with the West. But I am determined to change that."
Edmonton Journal, October 14, 1990

On seeking the support of cranky western malcontents seven years later

"Yes, Premier Clark was right, the federation does not

work for British Columbia and for every other region. Maybe not . . . maybe not 100 percent of the time to 100 percent satisfaction, but a country is more than a balance sheet."

Liberal fundraising speech, Vancouver, October 2, 1997

"[British Columbia is] rich, why? Because you're the door to the Pacific. Because you're part of Canada. The wealth of the country is the wealth of [the country]. This province is doing very well at the moment. Very well. . . . Do you think the leader of an independent B.C. will force the American president to his knees?"

Vancouver Sun, October 4, 1997

On seeking the support of cranky western malcontents eight years later, after creating a special caucus task force to find out why the Liberals were stuck in Western Canada's doghouse

"Too often these days, Western Canadians are unfairly characterized in the media and by opposition parties as uniformly alienated and disenchanted."

St. Catharines–Niagara Standard, January 1, 1999

On seeking the support of cranky western malcontent ten years later

"I consider Calgary as a second . . . second city for me.

Alberta is my second province. . . . My connections are pretty deep with this province, and I have always felt very comfortable in Alberta."

March 23, 2000, Liberal fundraising dinner, Calgary, quoted in the *National Post,* January 27, 2001

On maintaining close ties with cranky western malcontents

"[I like to] do politics with people from the East. . . . [Stockwell Day and Joe Clark are] from Alberta. They are a different type. . . . I'm joking—I'm serious."

National Post, November 23, 2000

On the Chairman's continuing bewilderment over cranky western malcontents

"You know I have traveled in the west a lot. I keep traveling there—I go there regularly. In fact my mother's family's from Alberta, but nobody knows it there and uh, but, the 400 cousins who live there, and uh, so, but, the reality's we made progress.

"Of course, it's the big title in the press. For my party we didn't, never did well there. Since Louis St. Laurent, we will elect some members and we lose them in the election after that. Many elections the only elected person was the francophone from St. Boniface, Manitoba, and we have nobody else. So for me, my party has done better. My Liberal party, since we're there, we—first election we had 26 Members, and it's the first time that we have re-elected 17 in the west and other times 17. I wish I would have a lot more, but it don't work for us. . . .

"In fact we are the only party—and I'm very happy that, that we have managed in the first time that the Liberal party three times in a row managed to have Members in every western province elected, and have Ministers who have been in the Cabinet since two terms being re-elected. . . . But there is a tradition, too, and I guess we're doing better than the Alliance is doing in Quebec, so that's another reality.

"And so, but for me, it's a national party, and there is some observers say that when they are—when you ask even in the west, when they look at the national picture, they'd like to vote for us. They think we're good nationally, but they don't believe that we have a local interest for them, so it's why they vote locally. . . . But [the West] seems to not believe we want their progress, economic progress.

"And the reality is the richest part of Canada is Alberta, and it's, and they've become extremely rich under Liberal government but never voted for them. . . . Something will break in, or somebody else, ten years from now. . . . [laughter from audience] I'm joking here."

Remarks at Duke University, North Carolina,
December 3, 2000

On persuading cranky western malcontents to see the big picture

"I was confronted with the same problem in Quebec. . . . I used the tough love theory in Quebec and I still have a lot of scars on my political body for that. . . . So I'm not discouraged in the West. . . . It's possible but we have to ask them to look at the national scene from a national perspective."

National Post, December 23, 2000

On finally coming to understand cranky western malcontents after all these years

"The reality is that they might not be comfortable philosophically with the Liberal Party, and this has nothing to do with because I am from the East. It is because they think we are too centrist and they like to have right-wing governments."

National Post, December 23, 2000

On Practicing Politics

"Politics is the art of walking with your back against the wall and your hands in front of your face and a big smile."
Straight from the Heart, 1985

On how to win at politics

"In order to win we have to create the impression that we are winning."
Chrétien: The Will to Win, 1995

"I've been up and I've been down. What's important in politics is to peak at the right time."
1992, quoted in the *Montreal Gazette,* March 16, 2000

"We'll either win, and win big, or we'll lose and have a hell of a time doing it."
1992, quoted in *Maclean's,* October 18, 1993

On being a Liberal politician

"They know that I'm a Liberal and they know that the Liberal mentality is very different from the Tory mentality, because the Tory mentality is oriented to serve the big business interests."

Ottawa Citizen, January 11, 1993

"Don't try to label me. Sometimes I side with the Left, sometimes with the Right."

Chrétien: The Will to Win, 1995

"Nobody can use my party for either only pro-choice or pro-life."

Globe and Mail, August 7, 1993

"I'm not doctrinaire, I'm a Liberal."

Victoria Times Colonist, July 7, 1992

On Conservative leader Kim Campbell's suggestion that an election campaign was not the right time to discuss policies in detail

"For the prime minister to say we should not talk about serious matters in an election . . . is almost contemptuous of citizens."

Alberta Report, October 25, 1993

On discussing the Chairman's policies in detail during an election campaign

"Let me win the election and after that you come and ask me questions about how I run the government."

Alberta Report, October 25, 1993

On a vote is a vote is a vote

"'Sir,' I said in my broken English, 'I am told you have decided to vote Liberal for the first time in your life. Would you please tell me the reason?'

"'Yes,' he barked. 'Because that guy Trudeau will put those goddam frogs in their place once and for all!'

"I wasn't quite sure how to answer, so I said, 'Thank you very much.' I slipped away and just let him vote Liberal."

Straight from the Heart, 1985

On whether the Chairman should reduce the GST

"I don't know. It is not what is politically smart, it is what is right for the nation, and what is right for the nation is always politically smart."

Canadian Press, October 16, 1997

On the shadows that political experience cast

"[Politics] is the only profession I know of where they believe a lack of experience is a great asset. It's like saying they never had a car accident when they have never driven a car."

New Brunswick Telegraph Journal, June 12, 1991

On reasons for calling an early election in the fall of 2000

"The opposition parties are already campaigning. They have asked for the election. Mr. Day dare me to call an election. . . . And I'm not to go to the people and say to them, I'd like somebody else to win. So, of course, I'm calling an election, hoping to win."

Sunday Report, CBC TV, October 22, 2000

On having a political motto

"My view of politics is, you always do your best, and at the end of the day you've done your best."

Globe and Mail, December 24, 1998

On Shooting Straight from the Lip

"Listen, I am a politician. Can you guarantee me I will be Prime Minister for the next 20 years? Great!"
The National, CBC TV, December 10, 1996

(Exchanging views with Canadian voters during a CBC TV/Radio Canada Town Hall Meeting)

On unemployment

Lori Foster, Regina, Saskatchewan: "I have three university degrees. I have spent four years looking for work. . . ."

Chrétien: "But, in fact, you live in the province where you have the lowest level of unemployment."

Foster: "That hasn't helped me."

Chrétien: "And some people, unfortunately, like you, find it very difficult to find a job. Some are lucky, some are unlucky, and that's life. . . . If your specialty does not lead to give you a job in Saskatoon, perhaps you can go to Regina or elsewhere. But I'm not living there."

On government waste

Marie-France Geoffroy, Quebec City, Quebec: (translated) "What I find depressing is to see my money blown away on things like my MP's pensions, the Senate, the army, and a private room for a criminal waiting for an operation. It makes me sick when I think of it. I have a feeling that honest people are being hurt. . . ."

Chrétien: (translated) "You say 'abolish the Senate.' I could abolish it tomorrow. I am not that keen on it. But we need the consent of the 10 provinces to do so or even to make an elected Senate. But every time we put the issue on the table, some people say, 'We will say yes if you give us something else.'"

On health care

Marie-France Geoffroy: (translated) "Being self-employed, I also have to think about my future, about my retirement. When I plan my budget must I think that my grandchildren will have to rely on me to pay for their hospital costs or for them to get health care in the United States because all our doctors will have gone there?"

Chrétien: (translated) "Well, I am sorry, but I think the Canadian universal health care system, which guarantees access to hospital, regardless of how much money you earn, will remain."

Jean-François Lepine, Host: (translated) "You can guarantee her that?"

Chrétien: "Listen, I am a politician. Can you guarantee me I will be Prime Minister for the next 20 years? Great!"

On Quebec separation

Howard Miller, Gaspé Bay, Quebec: "In such an event [as Quebec secession], could [anglophone Quebecers] expect any assistance, financial or otherwise, from our Canadian government in that disastrous scenario?"

Chrétien: "Yeah, but I do not want to spend a lot of time on the disastrous scenario."

Miller: "Excuse me . . . prior to the last referendum, you also said that you did not want to spend a lot of time on the scenario. We came within one percentage point [of losing]. . . . I'm asking you right now, for my fellow anglophone Quebecers, what type of contingency plan is in place in the event Quebec does separate?"

Chrétien: "For me, I just say that the goal of this government is to make sure that if there is a referendum, that it will be won. We are proposing some changes at this time. You saw yesterday, for example, the reaction of most of the premiers—quite positive to recognize the fact, that in fact, Quebec is a different society. You know that."

Miller: "Based on your answer, I can assume that we will be abandoned then."

Chrétien: "No, because we will fight for you. We're fighting for you."

Peter Mansbridge, Host: "Yes or no, on his question. Is

there, or is there not, a contingency plan to protect anglophone Quebecers who want protection in the case of a yes vote; just yes or no. If there was a contingency plan, would you tell us?"

Chrétien: "The problem is you're putting me a hypothetical question to the limit."

Miller: "It's not hypothetical with a one percent differential."

Chrétien: "Yes sir."

Miller: "No sir, it is not."

CBC TV, December 10, 1996

"A few days ago I kissed the floor, like the Pope, on behalf of the Kosovars, and they said I fell. . . . But you have to understand the people of Canada like a Prime Minister who is down to earth."

Calgary Herald, May 14, 1999.

On the Chairman's decision to go skiing at Whistler rather than attend the funeral of King Hussein of Jordan

"If, like President Clinton, I had a Boeing 747, I would have been able to go there nonstop, but we do not have a plane like that for the prime minister of Canada to allow us to travel throughout the world. . . . There was no miscalculation, nobody knew when it was to happen and I was not to stop to wait for him to die, so I am sorry that I could not make it and I expressed such a view to the ambassador, who understood."

National Post, February 10, 1999

On the morality of judging other countries' morals

"It would be very presumptuous for Canadians to tell other people how to conduct their morals. I remember a few years back in this House where we were telling the people that the government had no business in the bedrooms of the nation. The people in my riding complained and told me I was approving homosexuality. . . . So I cannot impose my morality on adults in the bedrooms of Canada, I do not see how I can go to another country and judge their morality."
Hansard, December 1, 1976

On the Chairman's friendliness with Chinese Premier Li Peng of Tiananmen Square infamy

"I don't receive flowers from men very often in my life."
November 28, 1996, quoted in the *Edmonton Sun,* April 14, 2000

On might over rights

"The press wanted me to give instructions to the Chinese. I said we have to put it in perspective a bit. You know we are 30 million. They are 1.2 billion. They want me to tell the Chinese what to do, but they don't want me to tell the premiers what to do."
Calgary Herald, February 13, 2001

On the execution of Nigerian democratic leader Ken Saro-Wiwa in November 1995

"I met myself the son before the hanging of—I forgot his name, but he has a complicated . . . Anyway I met his son and we tried to prevent the execution of this gentleman."

G-7 Summit, Lyon, France, quoted in the *Ottawa Sun*, July 7, 1996

On the occasion of a news conference with the United Nations Commissioner of Human Rights, Mary Robinson, when the Chairman was asked about the imminent execution in a Texas prison of Canadian Stan Faulder, which Canada was challenging

"I have no comment."

Ottawa Citizen, November 28, 1998

On hearing Commissioner Robinson's informed, detailed and gracious reply to the same questions regarding Canada's *amicus curiae* brief to the U.S. Supreme Court

"Here, I voted against it in Canada and we don't have the death penalty. But I don't know anything about this specific problem that they're asking me. You do, good for you. Merci beaucoup."

Ottawa Citizen, November 28, 1998

On the Chairman's sense of direction regarding the Middle East peace process when asked why he did not visit disputed East Jerusalem

"I don't know if I am in West, South, North or East Jerusalem right now. I came here to meet with the prime minister and here I am."

Calgary Herald, April 10, 2000

On the geo-political complexities of Israeli–Syrian diplomacy regarding the Sea of Galilee

"I understand the need for Israel to keep the only lake they have."

April 11, 2000, quoted in the *Edmonton Sun,* April 14, 2000

On whether he would recognize a unilateral declaration of statehood by Yassar Arafat if negotiations with Israel failed

"We think that the solution is to keep [a unilateral declaration of independence] part of negotiations because that puts pressure on both parties to come to a resolution. . . . This possibility is there. It's an element that will incite the parties to an agreement. . . . It's better to keep it as a pressure point for the negotiations—that's the position of Canada."

Toronto Star, April 11, 2000

On being reminded that Jacques Parizeau had planned a unilateral declaration of independence if the separatists won the 1995 referendum

"Quebec is not occupied territory, Quebec is not a colony—it's a province of Canada."

Toronto Star, April 11, 2000

On Making Promises to Keep

"There will not be a promise that I will make in the campaign that I will not keep."
September 10, 1993, quoted in
Maclean's, September 20, 1993

On unveiling his first famous Red Book at the beginning of the 1993 election campaign

"You can come with this book in front of me every week after I'm the Prime Minister and say, 'Where are you with your promises, Mr. Chrétien?' And we are going to check—I'm telling you everything that is written there I intend to implement."

Toronto Star, September 16, 1993

"I say there are no tax increases in this plan [the Red Book]. I said in an interview the other day, if we were to be in a war—perhaps."

1993 election campaign, quoted in the *Toronto Sun,* February 24, 1997

"Canadians have reached the saturation level with respect to taxation. . . . I don't see how we will be able [to raise them]."

Toronto Star, March 27, 1993

On being reminded of his "no tax increases" promise after raising taxes 62 times between 1994 and 2000 and collecting $6 billion per year from people living below the poverty line

"Yes, we have changed some taxes because we plugged some loopholes that were benefiting the rich. Yes, of course we have increased some taxes."

Hansard, February 11, 1997

"I say there are no tax increases in this plan . . . if we were to be in a war—perhaps."

On Scrapping the GST

"I am opposed to the GST. I have always been opposed to it, and I will always be opposed to it. It is a tax that is both regressive and discriminatory."
October 28, 1990, Speech at a Liberal fundraising brunch, Montreal, quoted in the *Globe and Mail,* October 29, 1990

On the intricacies of GST reform

Question: "I'm sort of confused on this GST business. On the one hand, you say you'd kill it by using the Senate."
Chrétien: "Yes."
Question: "On the other hand, you're not willing to say that there'll be some sort of GST should you take office. What are you saying to the Canadian public?"
Chrétien: "You will never see the same GST if we form the government."
CBC *Newsworld,* September 17, 1990

"We could be repealing the GST altogether. It will not

stay this way because it is unfair this way. Some services should never be taxed."

Halifax Chronicle Herald, October 22, 1990

"A Liberal government would . . . remove the Goods and Services Tax on reading materials."

Letter to the Don't Tax Reading Coalition, September 1992

"But the commitment we've made to the public is we want to get rid of the GST. I've always said the GST will go."

CTV News, January 22, 1993

"If the GST is not gone, I will have a tough time, the election after that. It's the only specific promise that I'm making very clear, and it is going, it's gone."

CBC Prime Time News, February 11, 1993

KEEPING THE GST

"Sometimes, in the course of a mandate, you're faced with a situation where you cannot deliver. . . . You have to have some flexibility . . . because acts of God come in the administration. And no politician can see everything happening."
Globe and Mail, May 3, 1996

On the need for Canadians to understand the fine print (dialogue from a CBC TV/Radio Canada Town Hall)

Johanne Savoie, Montreal, Quebec: "When I voted for you, I voted for you—I didn't read the Red Book. I voted for you, based on your promise to repeal the GST. And you did not."

Chrétien: "Did you read the Red Book on that? It's not what we said in the Red Book. You should have read it."

Savoie: "You were saying in all your speeches that you were promising to repeal the GST."

Chrétien: "We always said that we were to harmonize the tax with the provincial government, and we have done it with the Quebec and the Maritime provinces.

We never said it was to be repealed. Read the Red Book. It was written quite clearly."

Savoie: "What we heard during the campaign, for those of us who didn't read the Red Book, and that's most of us, was that the GST was going to be repealed."

Chrétien: "No, no. We said that we were to harmonize the taxes to have a better system because of the duplication that existed. . . . but we never said in the Red Book, or directly, that it was to be scrapped."

Savoie: "I didn't hear simpler—I heard scrapped."

Chrétien: "From whom?"

Savoie: "From you on television and on the radio."

Chrétien: "When?"

Savoie: "During the campaign. This is what I heard. Maybe they should pull tape. I don't know."

CBC TV, December 10, 1996

(What was discovered when CBC reporter Neil MacDonald "pulled tape")

"The odds of the GST surviving the next elections, are no better than the odds of the Mulroney government being re-elected."

CBC file footage, October, 1990

"The commitment we have made to the public is we want to get rid of the GST."

CBC file footage, December 1992

Announcer: "Will you abolish [the GST]?"

Chrétien: "Yes, I will abolish it."
CFRB Radio interview, August 1993

"We hate it and we'll kill it."
CBC file footage, May 1994

On the illusion of confusion

"The expression of the government was confused. For me, I was always careful. In all the statements I always said we have to find a new way to replace that tax. The confusion came from the fact that a lot of people in the land thought that we were to abolish the GST and nothing else. . . . "
CTV National News, December 13, 1996

On the media's role in confusing the public about the GST

"But you pick up a phrase of 50 words and you take three out of it."
CTV National News, December 13, 1996

On the Chairman's new appreciation of public sentiment about the GST

"If I and others left the impression with anyone that we would be able to do away with the tax without a replacement, I want to tell them that I am sorry."
Ottawa Citizen, December 17, 1996

On the Chairman's admitted flexibility regarding the GST

"The difficulty we had in the last recession is that the [Mulroney] government was obliged to raise taxes in the middle of the recession—and they had no choice and I don't blame them—but the situation was that way."

National Post, January 30, 1999

On Waging War

"I'm not a pacifist but we should not be at war."
Globe and Mail, February 14, 1991

On the American invasion of Panama

"I would have said [the invasion of Panama] was wrong. I understand [the Americans'] frustration but there is a rule of law in the world that has to be fundamentally respected. . . . Who knows if one day there might not be a President frustrated with us?"

Financial Post, June 30, 1990

On the Gulf War

"Mulroney has committed our troops there because he likes to be friends with George Bush. . . . I don't want to be friends with George Bush."

Toronto Star, January 12, 1991

"The reality is that we're debating war tomorrow and our answer is no."

Globe and Mail, January 15, 1991

"If faced with an act of war, we say on this side of the House that it is premature and that our troops should not be involved in a war at this moment and our troops should be called back if there is a war."

Hansard, January 15, 1991

"We say that it is not the time for war and that there are other means such as sanctions, embargoes and diplomacy."

Hansard, January 15, 1991

On the Gulf War one week later

"In order to get [Saddam Hussein] out of Kuwait, you have to crush him."

Toronto Star, January 23, 1991

"The NDP position is crazy and makes no sense. There is no such thing in a war like a defensive role. The CF-18 are not being built to distribute milk . . . and these Canadian soldiers are not being trained to be the Red Cross. They are part of war."

Remarks to Sikh community, Victoria, February 4, 1991

"When you play hockey you go on the ice and not sit in the stands and applaud. You get out there and fight."

Remarks at the University of British Columbia, February 4, 1991

On renewed tensions in the Gulf in 1998

"We support the bombing. Saddam Hussein got what he should have expected to get."

Vancouver Sun, December 17, 1998

On the Tory government plan to replace aging military helicopters, which the Chairman cancelled when elected

"I'm sure when the cabinet made that decision that day, probably all the ministers—not only Charest and Campbell—who were smoking pot. . . . It makes no sense when we see so much poverty in the streets. . . . [Reporters then asked Chrétien if he had smoked pot.] I don't smoke cigarettes, I should start there first. . . . I don't know what it is . . . have you got some?"

Toronto Star, April 3, 1993

On THE ECONOMY

"GM, Ford and Chrysler spent more money for the health programs of their employees than they spend on steel, so that in Canada, you know, if you're competing with the United States, uh, you have your steel for free."
Remarks at Duke University,
North Carolina, December 3, 2000

On worker productivity

"You don't increase productivity with speeches and say, 'I will increase productivity.' We have to motivate the people to improve productivity."
CTV Question Period, June 3, 1984

On workers in industries vulnerable to liberalized trade

"I want these people to be afraid of losing their jobs, it's the best motivation in the world."
Le Soleil, July 15, 1978

On those people who were afraid of losing their jobs and did

"Certainly there are too many unemployed, but the unemployment rate today isn't what it was 25 years ago. Today, we'd rather see a guy at home getting two-thirds of his salary [on unemployment insurance] than have him doing useless work, like opening doors for people who could just as well open them themselves."

Le Soleil, July 15, 1978

On the benefits of a stable unemployment rate

"For the first three months in the news this week, unemployment remained, you know, did not go up, remained at 8.4 percent. We have around one-percent inflation. A few weeks ago, there was a report that for the first time in a long time, the Canadian, the productivity in Canada, has been higher than the Americans. Americans. It's all a very positive sign.

Ottawa Citizen, September 12, 1998

On creating employment

"Work is created by the creation of jobs."

Saturday Night, November 1997

"But I don't believe I can be a Santa Claus. I'm not a

maker of illusions. There's not some magic solution to get rid of unemployment."

Toronto Star, November 22, 1978

On bolstering the economy with the Chairman's infrastructure program

"When a mayor decides to build a bridge, fix a sidewalk, you know it is not for a week. It is for years to come. And when they will do the work, everybody travels in the cities and when they see some workers, how they're busy, trucks moving, you see things are not that bad."

CBC Prime Time News, December 29, 1992

On concerns that provinces and municipalities might not be able to afford their two-thirds share of the cost of the Chairman's infrastructure program

"That's their problem."

Alberta Report, October 25, 1993

On the continuing danger of inflation

"I have said consistently that inflation remains a threat to us."

Speech to the Canadian Club, Montreal, February 27, 1978

On the continuing danger of regarding inflation as a continuing danger

"No policy caused more damage to the Canadian economy than [the Conservatives'] zero inflation obsession . . . [which was a] macho monetary policy."

Speech to the Empire Club, Toronto, February 11, 1993

On the economic stimulus provided by immigration

"They get off the boat and the first thing they do is buy a house, they buy a car. . . ."

Alberta Report, October 25, 1993

On government initiatives to balance regional disparity

"Without [government] incentives, everything will tend to become concentrated in the industrial heartland of central Canada. Already the stretch from Oshawa to Hamilton in Ontario is one big town, and it won't be long before Torontonians will have to decide whether to drive or fly when they are invited out for cocktails."

Straight from the Heart, 1985

On payroll taxes as an impediment to job creation, speaking less than two years before introducing a 73 percent increase in Canada Pension Plan premiums

"We believe high payroll taxes are nothing more than a tax on hiring."

Hansard, February 14, 1995

On high Employment Insurance payroll taxes creating a huge "surplus" in the EI fund

"When we took over the unemployment insurance fund it was billions of dollars in the red. We put it in the black."

Hansard, October 7, 1997

Free Trade (while in opposition)

"We'll eventually lose the freedom of making decisions for Canadians in Canada. . . . What that means is we're selling the store."
St. John's Evening Telegram, February 25, 1988

On Canada becoming the next American state

"Sometimes I wonder why we persuaded Quebecers to remain Canadians when some people now threaten to lose our identity from sea to sea. . . . The error of the Parti Quebecois was to hold a referendum. I wonder if the problem is now being presented exactly the other way: If the links that this government is trying to create with the United States won't mean that we will become Americans without ever giving our consent."
Globe and Mail, June 10, 1986

"What worries me is . . . that, in deciding for perhaps short-term gains that are not yet visible, we might come so close to the American neighbor . . . that eventually we might just be part of the U.S."

Toronto Star, June 15, 1986

On the disadvantages of free trade for Canada

"We paid too much for too little."

Montreal Gazette, October 23, 1988

"It was not good for Canada, but Brian [Mulroney] needed a deal politically."

Canadian Press, October 31, 1988

On southern Albertans, who puzzled the Chairman by supporting free trade because he assumed they were resistant to new ideas

"Why are they voting for free trade? That's a big change. They should be the ones quarrelling with it. . . . It's a leap in the dark. You might end up on a rock or in the lake, but it's still in the dark."

Canadian Press, November 19, 1988

On the Chairman's approach to free trade

"We'll renegotiate free trade. The Americans will want to keep as much of it as possible. They won't want to negotiate because it's a good deal. They won't want to lose any of it. . . . But it's either renegotiate or they will lose it all so they will renegotiate."

Halifax Daily News, July 31, 1991

"A Liberal government would block all foreign takeovers that are not in the country's economic interests."

Toronto Star, June 25, 1991

On Free Trade (while in government)

"Some people think that the American culture is a problem. It's not a problem. . . . Don't be afraid to be citizens of the world."
November 1993, quoted in *Maclean's*, January 8, 2001

On becoming a disciple of free trade

"Make no mistake about it, our government is committed to fast-tracking freer trade."
Speech to the Economic Club of New York, March 1997

On the advantages of free trade for Canada

"We were not against free trade as such, but we felt that the agreement as negotiated needed improvement. We were successful in that respect. I am pleased the system is working well."
Hansard, September 26, 1997

"I find it's worked very well. . . . Our trade with the United States has multiplied enormously and Canada has adjusted very well to the situation."

London Free Press, January 2, 1999

On Ross Perot's efforts to rekindle the Chairman's aversion to continental free trade

"What I recall very well is that a guy by the name of Perot called. . . . He told me that if I were to not go along [with NAFTA], 'We will build you the biggest monument to you in Texas that you've ever seen.' . . . [Perot] should have offered me a big factory in my district."

After the 1993 election, quoted in *The Selling of Free Trade,* 2000

On the Value of a Dollar

"A floating dollar floats."
Chrétien: The Will to Win, 1995

On the Canadian dollar plummeting to a record low of US$.63

"You know, the problem is that it is the market decisions. You know, either you know it's floating currency and, uh, it's monetary policy under the Canadian law like in most of the countries is managed by the Bank of Canada, and, uh, that's it.

"It's the way that the system operates, it's not the prime minister, it's the governor of the Bank of Canada who makes these daily decisions. . . . But, yeah, but I can personally—I am telling you that Canadian economy is functioning very well. . . . You know, we reduced the deficit from $42 billion to a surplus that was billions of dollars. . . .

"So, you know, not much I can say more than that and the, the monetary policy of the Canadian government and the Canadian people is made by the governor of the Bank under the Bank Act, Bank of Canada Act, not the Bank Act. Merci beaucoup. Thank you very much."

Ottawa Citizen, September 12, 1998

On the benefits of a weaker dollar

"I can live personally with a weaker dollar. I was there when it went from 93 cents down to 85 cents, and it was good for exports."

CTV Question Period, June 3, 1984

"In those days, I would like to tell [Prime Minister Trudeau,] the dollar went down when we were there because in Canada the paper mills were closed down, the mines were closed down, and it was the instrument I used to bring Canada back to a competitive position."

Hansard, October 10, 1991

"I can live personally with a weaker dollar."

"It was the instrument I used to bring Canada back to a competitive position."

On The Somalia Commission

"No one can say that it is not an inquiry which is independent, open and has all the resources."
Hansard, September 17, 1996

On allowing the independent Somalia Commission to be truly independent

"The time has come to let the Commission do its work."
Hansard, April 23, 1996

"We should let the commission of inquiry get on with its job. . . . Let the inquiry do their jobs. That is what they are there for and they should be allowed to do it."
Hansard, September 16, 1996

On the Somalia Commission's finding that it had identified at least two efforts to cover up wrongdoing, including the murder of a Somali teenager by Canadian soldiers

"I don't know what you are talking about. . . . Some things went wrong in Somalia, some guys have been taken to court. . . . But it's five years ago. The incidents happened before we formed the government."

Globe and Mail, July 4, 1997

On letting bygones be bygones by prematurely shutting down the Somalia Commission

"We have to run a government and we have an army and the morale was low and the army has done great things in Canada. . . . Yes, there was some mistakes made and it's normal in life. But now the time had come to move on and we did move on."

Toronto Star, October 18, 1997

On THE CHAIRMAN'S PAYCHEQUE

"I'm making less than the worst hockey player in the NHL."
CTV National News, February 4, 1998

On the concerns expressed by Michel Gauthier of the Bloc Quebecois that the Chairman was misusing Employment Insurance premiums

Gauthier: "Does the Prime Minister not realize that this choice [to use the EI surplus to reduce income taxes rather than improve EI benefits] does not make sense when he as Prime Minister could benefit from a tax reduction at the expense of the unemployed even though he pays no EI premiums?"

Chrétien: "Mr. Speaker, I am subject to the same payroll deductions as the leader of the Bloc Quebecois. I think that I pay EI premiums just as he does . . . [the Chairman is loudly informed by hecklers that MPs do not contribute to EI] At any rate, if we are not contributing, if I am not personally covered, it does

not bother me personally. . . . Why is the honourable member engaging in demagoguery when he is in the same boat? He is trying to blame the Prime Minister for a situation that also applies to himself and all the members of this House."
Hansard, November 4, 1998

On a challenge to trim the MP pension plan

"I don't think that the Members are overpaid. . . . Every member of this House who has been elected makes less than half of [what] the worst hockey player in the NHL [makes]."
Victoria Times Colonist, January 26, 1994

On the financial benefits of being Chairman

"No one comes here for the money. No one comes here for the working hours."
Reply to the Speech from the Throne, January 31, 2001

On the US$252-million contract offered to Alex Rodriquez by the Texas Rangers

"[George W. Bush] and I made a little calculation that it would take a long time for him and I to make that much money. I think it is 500 years of work."
Globe and Mail, December 15, 2000

On Never Losing the Common Touch

"I go to my constituency every month. Ask the people of Shawinigan, when I go to the shopping centre I sit with the people, I call them the old-timers' league, I sit with them and I talk to them. Sometimes I stop in the taverns."
Ottawa Citizen, December 19, 1996

On why mentally ill Canadians should prefer the streets to hospitals

"There's one place I go to [in] Ottawa regularly and every day there is a man who is, unfortunately, and obviously sick. We just sit with a chair at the corner of the street. . . . But 20 years ago a person like that was in a hospital. Today we'll let them live in society. . . . He is better to have a form of freedom like that than to be in a hospital where he will just be a number."

Ottawa Sun, October 17, 1996

On reports that the Chairman had "invented" this homeless friend

"I've [talked to homeless people] a few times in my life because I want to know the real problems of the people. . . . It is more difficult now with the RCMP to do that—to go on my own—because they don't let me do it. It's less fun too."

Toronto Star, October 18, 1996

On the rising cost of food

"If cabbage is too expensive for you, buy something else."

Victoria Daily Colonist, June 15, 1978

On 24 Sussex Drive as a model of subsidized housing

"Yes, it's a nice place. It's a good subsidized housing unit."

Maclean's, January 11, 1999

 Labour Relations

"We are taking steps as an employer to ensure that we [the federal government] are a follower, not a leader, in compensation practices."
Speech to the Ontario–Canadian Manufacturers Association, Toronto, June 5, 1978

On remembering how, as a young lawyer, he lost the Confederation of National Trade Unions as a client and had to work for the big corporate bosses

"It was a kind of ideological switch. . . . I was not good enough for the unions, but I was good enough to be against the unions."
Chrétien: The Will to Win, 1995

On Canadian workers' right to collective bargaining during a grain handler's strike

"It is very easy to say that we should settle these strikes, but I am still waiting to hear any Member on the other side tell me, or the House, that we should deprive these workers of the right to strike. I am not willing to do that. . . . Parliament gave them the right, and I believe in collective bargaining."

Hansard, March 19, 1975

On Canadian workers' right to collective bargaining sixteen years later, during a public service strike

"I want to ask the minister if he will do the right thing. The people of Canada are suffering today. They want an end to this strike. A very easy way to solve this problem is to appoint back to work and we will have peace in this country. Then we will be able to deal with the other fantastic problems of this nation."

Hansard, September 16, 1991

On the Shawinigan Handshake

"[He] should not have been there. . . .
If you're in my way, I'm walking."
Globe and Mail, February 16, 1996

On muscling Bill Clennett out of his way at a Flag Day in Hull, Quebec

"[Mr. Clennett] was right in front of me shouting and trying to block my way, so I took him out. . . . He was a lightweight probably because he was not very heavy—I just move him out."

Globe and Mail, February 20, 1996

"Every time I face a crowd I pay attention, because you never know. Look at what happened to the prime minister of Israel. They . . . lost him."

Winnipeg Free Press, February 20, 1996

"I was just walking with the police and I was shaking hands with kids and signing an autograph and suddenly somebody is blocking my way and shouting and I took him and I gave him to police and I kept going. That's it. . . . Generally speaking, I am not confronted because the police keep people a bit away, but he was right in front of me trying to block my way, so I took him out. . . ."

Winnipeg Free Press, February 20, 1996

On whether he would pay the bill to repair Bill Clennett's broken teeth

"His tooth? You mean his bridge. That's part of the infrastructure program."

March 8, 1996, quoted in the *Edmonton Sun,* April 14, 2000

On becoming less of a heavyweight in the future

"I guess that when I will be to another flag ceremony, the only thing I will hoist is going to be the flag."

Vancouver Province, March 8, 1996

On the case for mistaken identity

"The fact is that I was wearing these new sunglasses. I was not used to them and I could not see very well with them. And when this guy Bill Clennett jumped in front of me I thought he was John Nunziata, so I took him out."

Joking at a National Press Club Dinner, *Edmonton Journal,* May 6, 1996

On THE APEC INQUIRY

"Those who tried to break through the fences were acting against the law and the police reacted reasonably. . . . For me, pepper, I put it on my plate."
Canadian Press, November 27, 1997

On confusing the difference between pepper and pepper spray

"Usually it's the rubber chicken dinner, but when we come to the West we have beef. Sometimes we have pepper steak."
Liberal fundraising dinner, Winnipeg, October 9, 1998

On learning the difference between pepper and pepper spray

"I am sorry that some people had a problem with the police there. No one wished for that to happen and that is why there is an inquiry. . . . That is why I made the joke [about putting pepper on my plate], and I probably should not have made it. I did not know that there was a pepper spray."

Globe and Mail, September 23, 1998

On pepper spray as a humane instrument of crowd control

"In the past, [the RCMP] used all kinds of methods. Apparently, this was a new one that I didn't even know about. The MP claims that this can cause damage to the person. If she is still suffering, I am sorry about that. . . . Instead of taking a baseball bat or something else, now they are trying to use more civilized methods and that's why they had towels at the same time to help."

Globe and Mail, October 20, 1998

On whether his reference to the RCMP using baseball bats was appropriate

"I don't know. You know, use water cannon? Tear gas? Is it better? I don't know. . . . I've never been involved in that."

Ottawa Citizen, October 21, 1998

"Insensitive? No, I'm very sensitive because I want [the APEC commission] to look into the complaint. . . . I was just saying that in some countries there are more severe methods than those used by police in Canada. Just watch TV at night. . . . I was the minister who introduced the Charter of Rights and Freedoms."

Ottawa Sun, October 21, 1998

"I was the minister who introduced the Charter of Rights and Freedoms."

On learning the value of refusing comment

"I don't have to explain anything. . . . [The whole affair] was handled very well by the police."

St. Catharines–Niagara Standard, September 10, 1998

"I am standing proud . . . to tell you we have not been tarnished at all since the last five years we formed the

government, and we intend to carry on that way."
Ottawa Sun October 7, 1998

On explaining his remarks by finding a new baseball analogy

"Mark McGwire had a bad couple of weeks. He stopped hitting home runs [and] almost immediately they started asking questions: Can he make it? Does he have what it takes? Did he ever have what it takes? The same is true for prime ministers. Prime ministers are at the plate so often that they, too, have their share of strike-outs. . . . We can all sometimes have a bad couple of weeks."
National Post, November 4, 1998

On Solicitor General Andy Scott, who was overheard saying that the APEC Commission would pin blame on RCMP officer "Hughie" Stewart and absolve the Chairman

"I am very proud to have a man of his calibre and experience serving in my cabinet. . . . He has gone everywhere to advance the cause of the weakest in society."
Ottawa Sun, October 8, 1998

On Andy Scott's resignation

"It is because the Solicitor General day after day was attacked unfairly by the opposition."
Ottawa Citizen, November 24, 1998

On taking the heat as a good Chairman should

"[The Opposition] is only on the Vancouver incident [in Question Period.] That's their choice. For me, my cabinet colleagues were laughing, thanking me, 'You take all the flak, and we're scot free.'"

Globe and Mail, December 24, 1998

On the claim that the Chairman's office played a direct role in suppressing freedom of assembly and freedom of speech

"I'm offended when people say I tried to take away rights from Canadians. I'm the father of the Charter of Rights. I gave a lot of rights to natives and so on. But I hope that the commissioner will look into all that and find out. I'm not nervous."

Maclean's, January 11, 1999

On resisting an appearance before the APEC inquiry, where the Chairman would be under oath

"When a prime minister is in the House of Commons talking to the people of Canada and all the elected people of Canada, it's as good as having a Bible here. . . . I repeat, in front of the nation and in front of God if you want . . . I never discussed security with anybody in the RCMP."

Calgary Herald, October 27, 1999

"When a Prime Minister is in the House of Commons talking to the people of Canada . . . it's as good as having a Bible here."

On Democracy and Parliament

"Canadians feel alienated from their political institutions and they want to restore integrity to them. . . . They have had enough of the abuses of Parliament and the arrogance of government."
Toronto Star, January 20, 1993

On the difference between democracy and dictatorships

"You cannot say over and over that what you do does not matter, and that you are right and everyone else is wrong. That is not democracy—that is a dictatorship."
New Brunswick Telegraph Journal, October 13, 1990

On the difference between democracy and dictatorship within the Liberal party under the Chairman's leadership

"We have a party position. The party position will remain the same until I change it."
Toronto Star, February 16, 1991

"You know, you have to accept when you run for the party that there is a set of policies that make the core of what it is to be a Liberal or an NDPer or a Conservative."

Toronto Star, January 20, 1993

"In the party there will always be a minority who must accept the majority."

Hill Times, May 25, 1995

"To respond to your question on free vote, it's something that interests me a lot. But how to have . . . the difficulty that you have with it is that you have caucuses, you have a party that is the governing party and you need equation in policies and if you give every member a free vote the problem is the people have a sense that you have no leadership in the country."

CBC Prime Time News, December 29, 1992

On appointing candidates over the objections of local Liberals

"If I really need a candidate, I will name him or her. [It is] a very democratic power."

Victoria Times Colonist, January 9, 1993

On what women want

"I hope to do it [intervene to appoint women candidates] in less than nine ridings this time, but sometimes I have

to intervene and I will. . . . Women don't want privileges, they want the right to compete."
Canadian Press, March 9, 1997

On the Mulroney government's use of closure to shut down debate in the House of Commons

"I think we should let Members of Parliament speak their mind as long as possible. There are other means. You can extend the hours and so on, and you judge an administration by the number of closures they use. I find it scandalous, what they're doing, but it seems to be quite acceptable today and I don't like it."
Press conference, Ottawa, January 19, 1993

On the Liberal government's use of closure more times in seven years (68) than the Mulroney government in nine years (66)

"Of course, improvements can always be made but there should be no doubt that Canada's Parliament serves our country well."
Calgary Herald, February 1, 2001

On shutting down debate himself

"The problem is, you can't have debates until you die."
Canadian Press, October 16, 1997

On Friends and Foes

"Gee, Pierre, you'd better learn something about politics or you won't go very far."
Chrétien: The Will to Win, 1995

On Marc Lalonde

"Lalonde is very bright, very knowledgeable, and very good in debates, but he is poor in human relations at times, however pleasant he might appear at a cocktail party."

Straight from the Heart, 1985

On the economic newsletter published by former finance minister John Turner

"Just a gossip column you can have for 15 cents at a newsstand in Toronto."

Ottawa Citizen, December 22, 1978

On Quebec Liberal Premier Robert Bourassa

"Personally, I don't like fence sitters."
Montreal Gazette, May 19, 1984

On Mark MacGuigan

"I always felt that MacGuigan was too educated for his intelligence; he seemed to stumble over his degrees, and that hurt him as a politician."
Straight from the Heart, 1985

On Brian Mulroney

"Mulroney has the Midas touch in reverse . . . everything he touches turns to garbage."
Edmonton Journal, October 14, 1990

"When the popularity of the prime minister is equal to the size of his shoes, you wonder whether you should kick him."
Winnipeg Free Press, March 4, 1992

On Lucien Bouchard and Preston Manning

"You have Bouchard who wants to go, and the guy from the West tells them to go to hell."
Toronto Star, April 9, 1991

On the Alliance party

"You never know when there will . . . be a force that will come and appeal to the dark side of human beings."

Canadian Press, November 7, 2000

On Joe Clark

"He started out as Joe Who, and now perhaps he is Joe McCarthy."

National Post, February 21, 2001

Canada and Canadians

"Rather than being a melting pot, Canada is a country which permits every one of us to be what we are and still be good Canadians. . . . I'm a goddam pea-souper and proud of it."
Chrétien: The Will to Win, 1995

On the convenience of being Canadian

"[Canada is] the United States with none of the inconveniences."

Paris Match, quoted in the *National Post,* June 19, 2000

On the inconvenience of being the Chairman of Canadians

"I think, very sincerely, that we have become a nation of bitchers. You know, we complain all the time. . . . Many problems, such as language and separatism, will always be here."

Globe and Mail, September 23, 1982

On what Quebecers really want

"Our beer, our Ski-doos, and our hockey games."

Chrétien: The Will to Win, 1995

On what Canadians know for sure

"There are two things all Canadians know: One is that they live in the best country in the world and the other is that their province doesn't get its fair share."

Toronto Star, October 3, 1997

On what Canadians want for sure

"What Canadians want is an honest effort and teamwork. What they want are changes that will benefit people, not politicians or bureaucrats. What they want is progress, not turf wars. . . . What they don't want are pressure-cooker tactics, threats and ultimatums, tantrums and accusations, jealousies and posturing."

Ottawa Citizen, June 19, 1996

On scaling back the promise of the Chairman's political hero, Sir Wilfrid Laurier

"We will make this first decade of the 21st century, Canada's decade."

Reply to the Speech from the Throne, January 31, 2001

THE DIVINE RIGHTS OF KINGS AND CHAIRMEN

"I don't operate a government with polls."
Ottawa Sun, May 18, 1998

On a poll revealing that 87 percent of Ontarians believed the federal government should pay all victims of the tainted blood scandal

"I'm not in politics for public relations. I'm in politics to do the right thing. I always look at what is best."
Ottawa Sun, May 18, 1998

On the need to make constitutionally correct decisions

"A responsible government makes up its mind, does what it thinks is right, and if it is constitutionally wrong, it's for the court to decide."
CTV Question Period, February 15, 1981

On why the Chairman barred reporters from a luncheon speech for public relations executives moments before the food arrived

"It was a private meeting. It was not a speech for the media. . . . I said trust [the media] and if they make a mistake call them. I could hardly say that to you guys [the media]."

Winnipeg Free Press, September 14, 1998

On trees blocking the view at La Mauricie, an area in the future Chairman's riding that he was lobbying to have declared a national park

"If you [forest managers] don't cut those trees down, I will go and cut them myself."

Chrétien: The Will to Win, 1995

On being asked how, as newly appointed Minister of State for Finance, the future Chairman was doing

"You see that pile of papers? That is what my deputy minister wants. As soon as I get something I want, he will get something that he wants."

1967, quoted in *Maclean's*, October 18, 1997

THE LONGEVITY OF THE CHAIRMAN

"I am the leader until I resign. I resign the day I resign."
Vancouver Sun, November 16, 2000

On knowing when it is time to retire

"I don't have to make decisions. I am the leader."
Globe and Mail, December 24, 1998

"I'm running. So don't ask me when the time . . . of course, if tomorrow I was to die I would not be running. If I were to be paralyzed I would not be running."
National Post, March 14, 2000

On knowing when it is not time to retire

"One day last year my little grandsons said: 'Grand-papa, stay in politics long enough so we can vote for you at least once'—I can't refuse. I feel I am the object of too big a pressure."
Paris Match, quoted in the *National Post,* June 19, 2000

"I don't lose my step; I don't even take steroids. I just work harder and run faster."

National Post, February 10, 1999

On viewing a photograph of himself flying downhill on skis at Mont Ste. Anne

"Looked like a guy in good shape, didn't I?"

National Post, March 14, 2000

On knowing when to soldier on

"Every time I ask myself, should I run or not run. Sometimes you decide not to run, and you change your mind and you run. That's exactly what happened to me last time. I suddenly decided I like the job."

Calgary Sun, January 24, 2001

"I've been fighting for Canada all my life . . . and I'm just getting warmed up."

Reply to the Speech from the Throne, January 31, 2001